Dot.

...

Randi Zuckerberg

ILLUSTRATED BY **Joe Berger**

PICTURE CORGI

DOT.

A PICTURE CORGI BOOK 978 0 552 57152 4

First published in the United States by HarperCollins Children's Books 2013

Published in hardback in Great Britain by Doubleday. Simultaneously published in paperback

by Picture Corgi, imprints of Random House Children's Publishers UK

A Random House Group Company

This edition published 2013

1 3 5 7 9 10 8 6 4 2

Picture Corgi Books are published by Random House Children's Publishers UK,

61–63 Uxbridge Road, London W5 5SA

www.randomhousechildrens.co.uk

www.randomhouse.co.uk

Addresses for companies within The Random House Group Limited can be found at:

www.randomhouse.co.uk/offices.htm

THE RANDOM HOUSE GROUP Limited Reg. No. 954009

A CIP catalogue record for this book is available from the British Library.

Printed in Italy

To my son, Asher – thank you for teaching me that life isn't always about rushing forward and looking back but about taking time to stop and simply appreciate the journey

– R.Z.

For Charlotte, Matilda, Bea and Martha, xxx

– J.B.

This is Dot.

Dot knows a lot.

She knows how to tap . . .

to touch . . .

to tweet . . .

and to tag.

She knows how to surf . . .

to swipe . . .

to share . . .

and to search.

And Dot LOVES to talk . . .

and talk

and talk

and talk!

But now . . .

Dot's

all

talked

out.

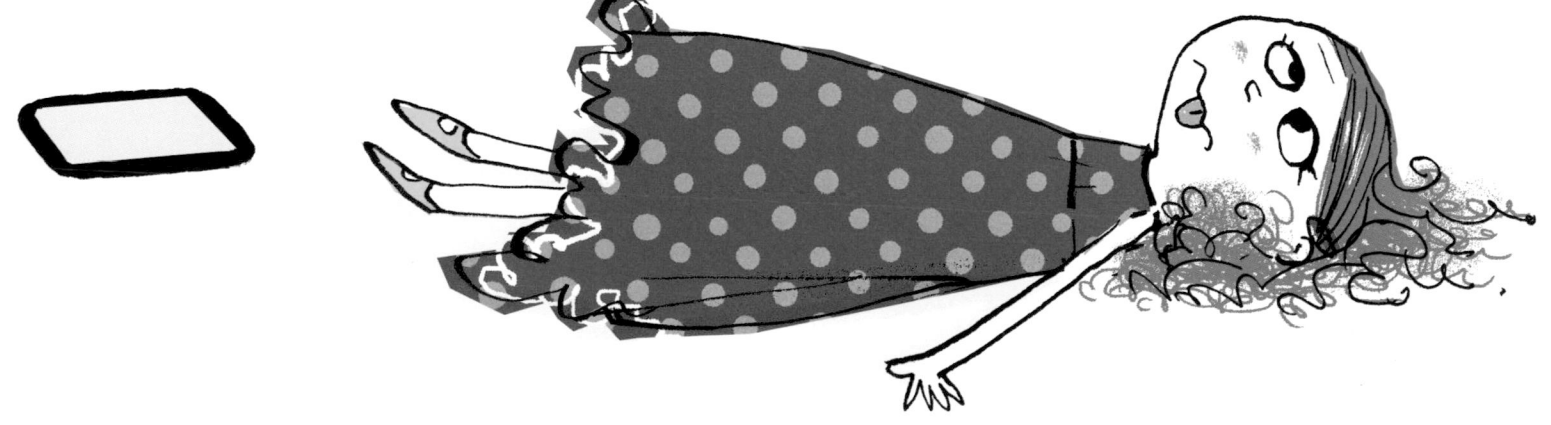

Mum says, "Go outside, Dot!
Time to
REBOOT!
RECHARGE!
RESTART!"

Outside . . .

Dot remembers . . .

to tap . . .

to touch . . .

to tweet . . .

and to tag.

Dot forgot . . .

she knows how
to surf . . .

to swipe . . .

to search . . .

and
to share.

Dot still loves to talk . . .

and talk
and talk
and talk!

This is Dot.

Dot's learned a lot.